John Joe
— and the —
Big
Hen

Martin Waddell
illustrated by
Paul Howard

WALKER BOOKS
AND SUBSIDIARIES
LONDON • BOSTON • SYDNEY

"It's your day for minding John Joe," Mammy told Sammy, so he had to stay with John Joe. Mary read her book and Mammy went on with her work. Splinter the dog sat in the sun and got toasted.

mped below.

THIS WALKER BOOK BELONGS TO:

_____

For Alison
~ **M.W.**

For the Millars
~ **P.H.**

First published 1995 by Walker Books Ltd
87 Vauxhall Walk, London SE11 5HJ

This edition published 1997

10 9 8 7 6 5 4 3

This book has been typeset in Granjon.

Printed in Hong Kong

British Library Cataloguing in Publication Data
A catalogue record for this book is
available from the British Library.

ISBN 0-7445-5243-5

Sammy got bored minding John Joe.
Sammy wanted to play with his
friend, Willie Brennan.
"I'm away down Cow Lane to the
Brennans'," Sammy told Mary.

"Take John Joe with you," said Mary,
but Sammy took Splinter instead
of John Joe.

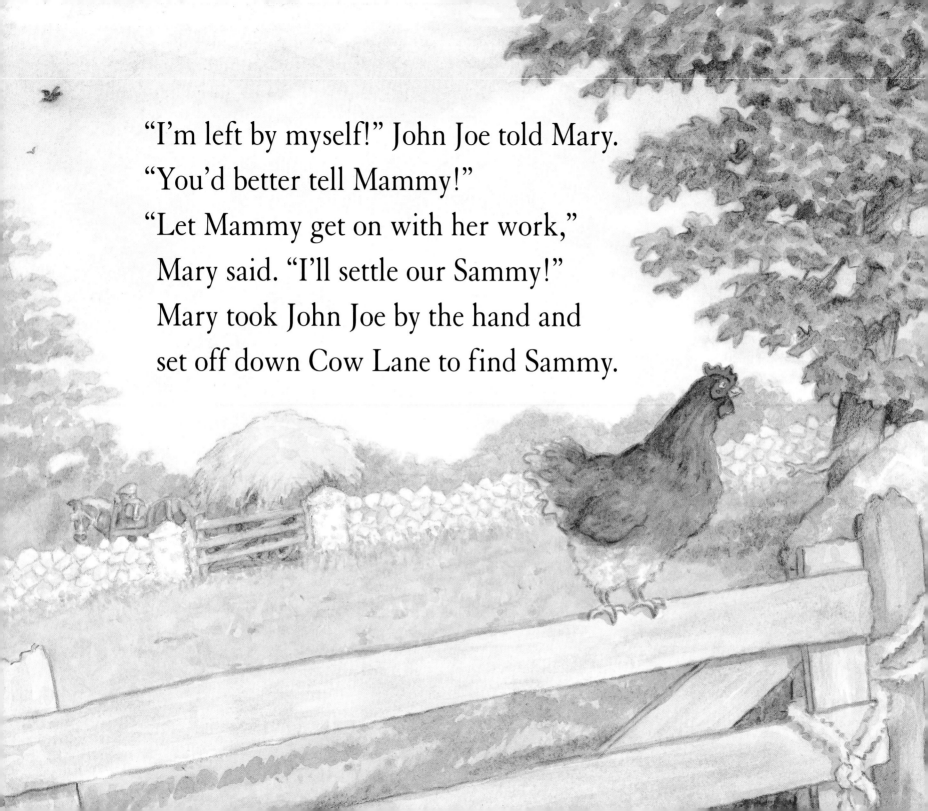

"I'm left by myself!" John Joe told Mary.
"You'd better tell Mammy!"
"Let Mammy get on with her work,"
Mary said. "I'll settle our Sammy!"
Mary took John Joe by the hand and
set off down Cow Lane to find Sammy.

They went to the Brennans', but there was no sign of Sammy! Mary was mad, for it wasn't her day for minding John Joe.
"Do you think they'd be down by the stream?" asked John Joe.
"I'd look, but you are too little to go," Mary said. "And I can't leave you here with no one to mind you."
"I'll mind myself!" said John Joe.

The Brennans' big hen came to
look at John Joe. John Joe was used
to the hens at his house, but he didn't
know the Brennans' big hen.
"I'm not scared of you!"
John Joe told the hen.
"I'll whack your backside,"
John Joe told the hen.

"Go away home, hen!"
John Joe told the hen …
but the big hen didn't go.

John Joe climbed on the wall,
for he thought that the Brennans'
big hen might eat him.

"MRS BRENNAN!" shouted John Joe,
but Mrs Brennan was out.

"MARY!" yelled John Joe, but Mary had gone after Sammy and she couldn't hear him.

"OH, MAMMY!" wailed John Joe, but Mammy was safe back at home.

That left John Joe alone with the Brennans' big hen and so . . . John Joe ran away from the hen!

Mary came back to the Brennans'
with Sammy and Splinter, but…

"Where's our John Joe?"
Sammy said.

"JOHN JOE!
JOHN JOE!
OUR JOHN JOE!"
shouted Sammy.

"JOHN JOE!"
shouted Mary.

No John Joe with the hens in the yard.

No John Joe with the pigs in the sty.

No John Joe in the ditch.

No John Joe in the barn.

"Go find John Joe, Splinter!" said Sammy.

Splinter walked round and sniffed
at the ground … and the wall …
and the top of the wall.
Then Splinter dived into the corn.
Splinter barked and he barked
and he barked…

WOOF! WOOF! WOOF!

John Joe was
asleep in the corn.

"The big hen chased me!" said John Joe.
"We thought you were lost," said Mary,
as she carried John Joe up the lane.

"John Joe was scared by the Brennans'
big hen," Mary told Mammy. "He hid
away in the corn. We thought that
we'd lost our little John Joe."
"There's no way I'm losing my little
John Joe!" Mammy said.

"It was your day for minding John Joe," Mary told Sammy. "Sure, I minded myself," said John Joe.